WHEN WILLY WENT

Written and illustrated
by Judith Kerr

Parents' Magazine Press / New York

TO THE WEDDING

First published in the United States of America
by Parents' Magazine Press 1973
First published in Great Britain
by William Collins Sons & Co., Ltd., London and Glasgow
Text and illustrations copyright © 1972 by Judith Kerr
All rights reserved. Printed in the United States of America

Library of Congress Cataloging in Publication Data

Kerr, Judith.
  When Willy went to the wedding.
  SUMMARY: No one wanted Willy's pets to attend his
sister's wedding but they came anyway.
  I. Title.
PZ7.K46815W13   [E]   72-8027
ISBN 0-8193-0658-4   ISBN 0-8193-0659-2 (lib. bdg.)

For my husband Tom

Once there was a boy called Willy.
He had lots of pets and a grown-up sister.
Willy's sister was so grown up that she was getting
married and Willy was going to the wedding.
"Shall I take my pets to the wedding?" said Willy.

"No," said Willy's father.

"No," said Willy's mother.

"No," said Willy's grown-up sister.

"Better not, old chap," said Bruce,
who was going to marry Willy's sister.
"Your pets might not like it."

So Willy did not take his dog to the wedding.
He did not take his cat or her three kittens.
He did not even take his goldfish.

He only took his hamster
because it liked to be in his pocket,
and his frog so that it would not be lonely.

"Come on!" said Willy's father.
"Everyone is waiting at the church."
It was not far.
"Remember to walk slowly," said Willy's father.
"And remember to hold up my dress,"
said Willy's sister.

The church was full of friends and uncles and aunts.
They all turned to look at the bride.
"I think I'll take a picture of the wedding,"
said Willy's Uncle Fred.

Suddenly one of the aunts pointed. "Look!" she cried.
It was not Willy's fault that his cat had followed
him to church. It was not his fault
that the three kittens had followed the cat.

"Cats don't come to weddings," said the vicar.
Willy said, "I'll look after them."
The vicar gave them something to sit on.
Then he married Willy's sister to Bruce.

"Now for the wedding picture!"
cried Willy's Uncle Fred.
Everyone stood quite still.
But Uncle Fred did not stand still.
It was not Willy's fault that his
dog was waiting outside the church.
It was not his fault that the dog
was pleased to see him.

"How disgraceful!" cried Willy's aunt.
"Take your pets home!" said Willy's mother.
"At once!" said Willy's father.
"I think they'd be happier there, old chap,"
said Bruce.

There was food and drink for everyone at home.
Willy said, "I'll give my pets something to eat."
The hamster was hungry too.

"Now I will take my picture of the wedding,"
said Uncle Fred.
But Willy's aunt screamed. "A mouse!
A horrible orange mouse!"

It was not Willy's fault that his hamster was hungry.
It was not his fault that the hamster liked cake.

And it was not Willy's fault that his frog wanted a drink…

...or that his aunt was frightened of frogs...

...or that the cats got all upset.

None of it was his fault, but everyone was cross.
"Take your pets away!" cried his mother.
"Right away!" cried his father.
"Away! Away! Away!" cried his aunt.

"But what about the picture?" said Willy.
"What about the picture of the wedding?
My pets should be in it.
After all they did all come."
"No!" said Willy's mother and Willy's father.
"No! No! No! No! No!" cried Willy's aunt.

Uncle Fred set up his camera.

"I'd better go then," said Willy.

But Bruce said, "Stop!"

Willy stopped.

"I don't agree at all," said Bruce.

"I am very fond of pets, and I should
love some in our wedding picture."

"Just a moment!" said Willy.

He ran to get something.

Uncle Fred clicked his camera.

It was a lovely wedding picture.

"I'm glad my goldfish wasn't left out," said Willy.
"Even a goldfish can enjoy a wedding."